This book is dedicated to everyone who has wished for and found
a best friend and home of their own,
for those who are still searching,
and especially for those who have created loving homes
filled with best friends creating families, assigned or chosen,
and
in loving memory of
Diane Marie McGowan
a single mom who taught me the importance of family
and the need to celebrate every day, usually with a hot fudge sundae.

Eleanor's Very Merry Christmas Wish

Written by Denise McGowan Tracy
Illustrated by John Michael Downs

First Edition: November 2020

ISBN 978-1-64663-302-9

Visit: www.eleanorswish.com

This is a work of fiction. With the exception of verified historical events (meaning none of it), all incidents, descriptions, dialogue, and opinions expressed are the products of the author's imagination and are not to be construed as real.

Published by

An imprint of

3705 Shore Drive,
Virginia Beach, VA 23455
800-435-4811
www.koehlerbooks.com

ELEANOR'S VERY MERRY CHRISTMAS WISH

DENISE MCGOWAN TRACY

ILLUSTRATED BY JOHN MICHAEL DOWNS

FOREWORD

My wish is that you'll make reading this book an occasion for yourself and for your family.
Please take the time to read it aloud surrounded by people you love who love Christmas
and all of the magic that surrounds this glorious season.

I hope you are transported to the wonder that is the North Pole
in all of its shimmering, glimmering joy.
Hot chocolate and cookies are optional, but a sense of whimsy is a must.

As you read, remember: wishes really do come true.
So, make YOUR wish!

CHAPTER ONE

THE NORTH POLE IS A MAGICAL PLACE

Hi, it's me, Twinkle. I hope you're in the mood for a story because I'd like to share with you one of my favorites. Before we begin, I think you need to know a few things about me. I believe in Christmas and everything it involves. The gatherings with friends and families. The search for just the right gift to make someone smile. The food. The fun. And the magic. But of course I believe in all of that. I'm an elf and I live at the North Pole. Pretty cool, right? I love my North Pole family. There's Santa, Mrs. Claus, Sprinkle, Sparkle, Clara, and all of the elves and the reindeer. Oh, and Eleanor, of course. She's not an elf. She's a rag doll. A most unique rag doll, and her story is very special indeed.

She has lived with us at the North Pole for a very long time. It's a wonderful story. So, where should I begin? Hmm . . . I know, how about I share some of the most special days I remember?

Yes, a typical day with Eleanor would find her just before lunch peering out her window and waving—probably at Sprinkle and Sparkle hurrying through the fluffy snow from the workshop on the way to lunch. Sprinkle runs Santa's workshop. And Sparkle is in charge of wrapping.

These are very important jobs at the North Pole. They would be especially happy today because Eleanor and Mrs. Claus made chicken pot pie for lunch.

Mmmmm, Eleanor thought, *chicken pot pie and oatmeal raisin cookies with milk for dessert.*

Eleanor needed to be on her way, too. Santa expected everyone to be on time when Mrs. Claus served her delicious meals. But Eleanor had to take one more peek out her window. She loved the way the snow looked when the afternoon sun was shining. It was bright and happy and magical—just like everything at her home in the North Pole. Santa was magical; Mrs. Claus was magical. The elves were magical. *Well, really,* Eleanor thought with a giggle, *it is the North Pole. Of course it's magical!*

Santa saw Eleanor in the window and smiled and gave her a wave as he made his way from the barn where he'd been checking on the reindeer. No matter how busy he was, Santa always arrived first at the table when Mrs. Claus served a meal. So, with a final glance in the mirror to be sure the ribbons were perfect on her braids, Eleanor ran to the kitchen.

Each and every day it was the same.

"Ho ho ho!" Santa said, as he stomped the snow off of his boots. "What is that delicious aroma?"

He walked into the cozy kitchen and gave Mrs. Claus a kiss on the cheek. Closely behind, Sprinkle came in and sat down at the end of the table with a big grin on his face until Sparkle said, "Ahem, Sprinkle, that is Mrs. Claus's chair!" Sprinkle jumped up with a surprised look on his face and said, "Oh gosh, it is?" Every single day it was the same scene, and they would all have a good laugh as Sprinkle held out the chair for Mrs. Claus to take her seat.

After lunch, Santa stood with his back turned—he thought nobody could see him—grabbed the plate of cookies, and said, "Well, one delicious cookie and then back to work."

Sprinkle laughed, pointed, and said, "ONE cookie, Santa?" as Santa headed out the door with a wink and a "Shhh."

CHAPTER TWO

SANTA'S WORKSHOP

After lunch, Eleanor joined the fun with the elves in the workshop. Everything looked so bright, shiny, and beautiful, and the sound of laughter filled the air. The machines the elves used to make the toys were as exciting as the toys themselves. The candy cane–colored wheels turned, and *whoosh!* Out came a shiny toy car. Over in the corner, the "Toyinator" made a whirring sound and then *whoosh!* Out came a brand-new bike.

Of course, not every toy was made by a machine. Many of them, especially the teddy bears, had to be made by hand. Each bear had to be as unique as the little boy or girl who received it. Santa and the elves had much to do to make wishes come true each Christmas morning.

This particular day was special indeed. As Eleanor entered the workshop, Sparkle asked, "Eleanor, would you like to help with gift wrapping today?"

Would she!

"Really and truly?" Eleanor asked. "Gift wrapping! I've never wrapped a gift before. Do you think I could?"

"Of course," replied Sparkle. "I mean, 'really and truly.' I'll teach you myself."

The gift-wrapping station exploded with color—shelves and shelves of shimmering, glimmering wrapping paper. And the ribbons . . . every single color in the whole wide world. Red and green and blue and silver and gold and purple and—Eleanor's favorite—pink! Some ribbons were wide and some were skinny, and some were sparkly with glitter and some curled . . . and they all made the prettiest bows. Oh yes, wrapping presents next to Sparkle and the other elves was exciting. Eleanor felt nervous at first, but the elves reminded her that they had been wrapping gifts for a long time and that soon she would be just as efficient as they were. The elves were patient with Eleanor, teaching her exactly how to pick the right amount of paper, how to fold the paper, how to crease it, how to tape it, and then, of course, how to flip it over to tie the bow.

As the tower of gifts grew taller and wider, Eleanor looked at Sparkle and said, "Gosh, Sparkle, the gifts are so beautiful. Wouldn't it be great if nobody opened them and they could stay this beautiful forever?"

"Hmm, well, they are gifts," Sparkle said, "so it's what's inside that counts."

"Just like people, I'd say," Twinkle said.

"Hmm, just like people . . ." Eleanor said. "I guess. But I think it would be wonderful if on Christmas morning a little boy or girl would take just a few extra seconds to look at the pretty gift wrap and think about how someone took the time to make it so special."

"Not ME!" Sprinkle interjected. "I hope they tear off the paper really, really fast so they can see the toy we made for them."

"Sprinkle, I agree with Eleanor," Sparkle said. "I hope a child out there loves the beautiful wrapping when they see their gifts on Christmas morning and opens it ever so carefully."

"And recycles the paper, of course," Twinkle said.

"Of course!" they all echoed.

CHAPTER THREE

COOKIE'S KITCHEN

Most days Eleanor joined Mrs. Claus—affectionately known as "Cookie"—in the kitchen. Eleanor loved everything she did at the North Pole, but her very favorite thing was to help Mrs. Claus bake cookies. The aroma in the kitchen was the best thing ever. Vanilla and sugar and cocoa and cinnamon—*mmmm*. Cookie made sure that Eleanor knew how to make each and every one of her special cookies. There were chocolate-chip cookies, sugar cookies with sprinkles, peanut-butter cookies, molasses cookies, shortbread . . . and so many more. Eleanor couldn't believe how many different kinds of cookies Cookie could bake.

Today they baked sugar cookies with fun, colorful sparkly sugar on top.

"But perhaps with all of these cookies," Cookie said, "I'd better make us all a nice, healthy kale salad for dinner."

She looked at Eleanor, and they both nodded very seriously before they burst out laughing.

"Yes, I think these are my favorite," Cookie said, as she put the cookies into the oven.

"But you say that about all of the cookies we bake," Eleanor said.

"Well, they ARE all my favorites," said Cookie. "Who says you can only have one favorite—in cookies, or family, or friends, for that matter? They're all different. And they're all wonderful. How could you possibly choose a favorite?"

That made perfect sense to Eleanor.

Oh, you may be wondering why we here at the North Pole call Mrs. Claus "Cookie." Years ago, Eleanor pointed out that Mrs. Claus made so many cookies that "Cookie" should be her name. Mrs. Claus laughed, hugged Eleanor, and said, "That's perfect!" She insisted, from that day on, that Eleanor call her Cookie. Well, of course, the nickname stuck, and pretty soon everyone at the North Pole called her "Cookie," which made Eleanor feel very proud.

As she helped with the baking, Eleanor thought that Cookie was a perfect name. Not at all like her name: Eleanor. She never understood why she had such a serious name. It wasn't pretty like some of the girls' names that she had seen as she added the gift tags to the presents.

"Cookie," she asked, "everyone here has such beautiful names. Sprinkle. Twinkle. Sparkle. Clara. Shimmer. Glimmer. Everyone but me. I'm just boring old Eleanor with my boring brown braids and my boring plaid jumper. It just isn't fair."

Just then Santa appeared in the doorway. "Eleanor?" he said. "You think Eleanor is a boring name? Why, it's just the opposite, if you ask me. Old fashioned, maybe. But sometimes the old-fashioned things are the best. Yes, I think it's a perfect name. When you came to us, we knew there was no better name for you."

"That's right," agreed Cookie. "Why, you're named after one of the most wonderful women of all time: Eleanor Roosevelt! After dinner tonight, I'll tell you all about this remarkable woman."

"And," said Santa, "we've been getting lots of letters from little girls with old-fashioned names, like Sarah and Hannah and Charlotte. I'd say you're quite the trendsetter, my dear."

"Well, look at me," laughed Eleanor, striking a fashion-model pose. "I'm a trendsetter! Oh, thank you, Santa. Thank you, Cookie. That makes me feel so much better."

"Now run along. Aren't the reindeer waiting for you to play some reindeer games?" Cookie asked.

"Yes," Eleanor said. "Rudolph wants to play Red Light, Green Light. But the game never goes anywhere because he insists on being the caller. And with his nose, it's ALWAYS red light."

Cookie and Santa burst out laughing as Eleanor ran out to play.

CHAPTER FOUR

A VERY MERRY CHRISTMAS WISH

That night in her room, Eleanor thought about what Cookie and Santa had said. Why did they always say, "When you came to us?" They never, ever said that about any other toy. And no other toy stayed as long as she had. Each year, Sprinkle, Sparkle, and the elves checked Clara's Naughty-and-Nice List, matched the toys to the good little children, and sent the toys off to their new homes. So why was SHE still here? It didn't make any sense.

She heard a knock at the door.

"Yoo hoo, Eleanor! It's me, Sparkle. Can I come in? I have a fabulous new hair ribbon. I think it would look perfect in your hair!"

Sparkle entered.

"A sparkly new ribbon for my boring old hair on my boring old me? A doll nobody ever wanted?"

"Eleanor," exclaimed Sparkle, "you mustn't say that. Of course you are wanted. You are such an important part of our North Pole family. We all love it here. It's just perfect."

"Yes," Eleanor said. "It's perfect for you. You're an elf. You, Sprinkle, and Twinkle. You're elves. You are supposed to be at the North Pole. But I'm a doll. I'm supposed to be with a child that wishes for me. I'm sorry, Sparkle. I know this sounds selfish and awful, and I love you all so very much. But my wish—my very merry Christmas wish—is for a best friend and home of my own. Do you understand?"

"I do," Sparkle said. "I have Sprinkle, even though he drives me crazy. And Twinkle has Clara. Santa has Cookie. I think we all want a best friend of our own—someone we can count on."

"All of the other toys have a child who has wished just for them," Eleanor said. "How come nobody ever wishes for me?"

"I don't have the answer to that, Eleanor," Sparkle said. "I wish I did. It bothers me to see you so sad. But maybe wishing isn't enough. Maybe you have to do something."

"Do something?" Eleanor said. "Like what?"

"I'm not sure," Sparkle said. "Only you can decide what's right for you. But until something changes, I think we can all agree that beautiful new hair ribbons are always a good idea."

"Agreed!" replied Eleanor.

They both hugged and laughed and spent the evening trying out new ribbons. Eleanor felt much better knowing that she had such good friends.

CHAPTER FIVE

THE LETTERS!

Up here at the North Pole we don't need a calendar to know when December rolls around. That's when the letters start arriving. So many letters!

Every year it's the same: a roaring fire in the fireplace, cookies, and cocoa, and Santa, Cookie, Clara, Sprinkle, Sparkle, and me, Twinkle. Sparkle has the important job of listening very carefully as Santa decides what to bring each child. And, of course, Sparkle plans the beautiful gift wrapping.

But no decision can be made without Clara. She's Santa's cousin and in charge of the Naughty-and-Nice List.

Eleanor thought Clara was the most beautiful person she had ever seen. She had a great big smile, jet-black hair, the bluest eyes and the brightest smile. She wore lovely dresses made of red-and-green velvet with white fluffy trim and gorgeous hats. And white boots!

"Clara," Eleanor asked one day, "how can you wear white boots every single day and never, ever scuff them? I could never do that."

"Oh, I'll bet you could," Clara said, laughing. "You can do anything you set your mind to. Why don't we have you try on a pair of my boots tomorrow?"

"Really and truly?" Eleanor asked.

"Really and truly!" Clara replied, crossing her heart.

"And maybe one of your hats?" Eleanor asked.

"How about the white, fluffy one?" Clara asked. "That's my favorite."

"Mine too," Eleanor said. "I'm going to feel so beautiful."

"Oh, Eleanor," Clara said, "you don't need any of my things to feel pretty. You're the most beautiful Eleanor there is!"

"Thank you, Clara," Eleanor said, "but I would still like to try those boots!"

They had a laugh at that.

"Fun tomorrow, but tonight, back to work," Clara said. "Let's get back to this list!"

Everyone gathered around Santa as they read the letters together. Each year, Eleanor heard all the Christmas wishes, and then *poof!* Friends appeared in the workshop. It was fun for her to have new toy friends each year. She had time to get to know them before they went off to their new homes. She was so happy for them and tried not to be too sad for herself.

After Santa read the letter from a child, he asked Clara if they had been on their best behavior that year. Clara carefully reviewed her list. Most of the time she said, "Yes, Santa, Sean Patrick was a very good boy this year," or "Of course, Santa, Dani was a very good girl this year." But every now and then, she looked up from her list with a very sad expression, shook her head, and said, "I'm sorry, Santa. It looks like Michael did not have his best year. I think we should only give him one or two things from his list."

Santa would look very sad and then let out a soft, "Ho ho ho."

"Oh, Clara," he'd say. "Not Michael? That can't be. I think we better send Michael just what he asks for. I'm sure he tried his best."

Sprinkle and Sparkle would nod in agreement. And Cookie always thought it was a very good idea, too.

Clara would sigh.

"Santa!" she'd say. "Why do I even keep a Naughty-and-Nice List if you 'really and truly' believe that every child is a good child?"

"Clara, every child is a good child," Santa always said. "In their hearts. If they always listen to their hearts, they will always do the right thing. And if I didn't have you here, how could I possibly keep track of all of the adventures they've had each year—and all of those wishes. Your work is very important."

They'd all laugh at that and say, "Nothing ever changes." But deep down, they knew Santa was right, and that next year Clara would be able to tell Santa that Michael had indeed had a better year, and that would make Santa very, very happy.

As they read the letters, Eleanor looked around and wondered what would happen if a little girl ever wrote a letter to Santa asking for a rag doll. Eleanor would miss her friends so much.

Eleanor was so lost in that thought she nearly missed the letter Santa was sharing:

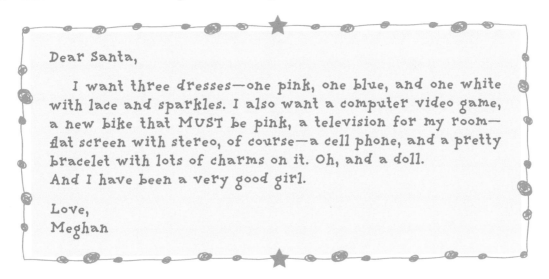

Dear Santa,

I want three dresses—one pink, one blue, and one white with lace and sparkles. I also want a computer video game, a new bike that MUST be pink, a television for my room—flat screen with stereo, of course—a cell phone, and a pretty bracelet with lots of charms on it. Oh, and a doll.
And I have been a very good girl.

Love,
Meghan

Santa put down the letter and looked at Eleanor.

"Well, that's quite a letter," he said. "What do you think, my dear? Meghan says she would like a doll."

"Oh no, Santa," Eleanor said. "She wanted so many other things before a doll. I need a little girl who really and truly wants me. And she didn't say 'please' or 'thank you,' and didn't even ask how you were doing or say to send a hug to Mrs. Claus."

"Yeah," said Sprinkle. "She didn't even ask about ME!"

"Or Clara. Or Twinkle," Sparkle said to an embarrassed Sprinkle, who realized just how silly and self-important he sounded.

"I need a child who 'really and truly' wants a best friend," Eleanor said. "Wants ME for a best friend."

Santa and the others nodded in agreement.

Santa looked at Sprinkle and said, "Yes, Eleanor is right. Let's send Meghan EVERYTHING on her list, except a doll. Oh, and, Sprinkle, let's send her a purple bike."

"But she asked for a pink bike," Sparkle said, looking confused.

"Yes, Sparkle, she did," Santa said. "Let's see how she handles that surprise."

"Check!" said Sprinkle, with a giggle. "One PURPLE bike for Meghan!"

CHAPTER SIX

WAITING. WISHING. WRITING.

That night, Eleanor began to "really and truly" believe that her wish would never come true.

Wait and wish, she thought. *Wait and wish. Wait . . . wait a minute! Maybe I shouldn't wait to get a letter. Maybe Sparkle is right. Maybe wishing just isn't enough. I should WRITE a letter.*

And with that, she walked to her desk, picked up her pencil, thought for a few minutes, then began to write.

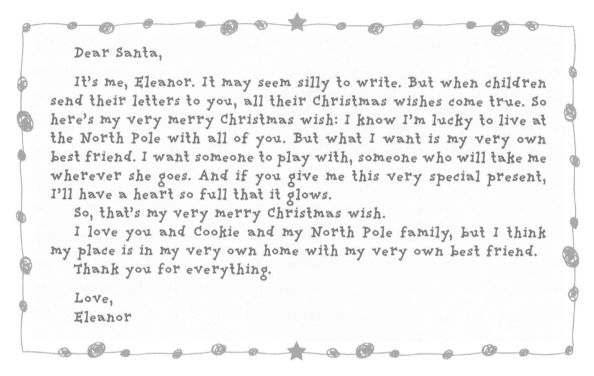

Dear Santa,

It's me, Eleanor. It may seem silly to write. But when children send their letters to you, all their Christmas wishes come true. So here's my very merry Christmas wish: I know I'm lucky to live at the North Pole with all of you. But what I want is my very own best friend. I want someone to play with, someone who will take me wherever she goes. And if you give me this very special present, I'll have a heart so full that it glows.

So, that's my very merry Christmas wish.

I love you and Cookie and my North Pole family, but I think my place is in my very own home with my very own best friend.

Thank you for everything.

Love,
Eleanor

Eleanor put the letter into an envelope, wrote "Santa" on the front, and tiptoed down the hall to put the letter at Santa's place at the table where he'd be sure to find it when he had his morning tea with Cookie.

At that very moment, thousands of miles away, there was a little girl named Noelle who also felt very lonely.

"Wait and wish!" Noelle said. "Wait and wish! I wait for the kids at school to talk to me. I wait for the kids on the block to ask me to play. Wait and wish. That's all I ever do."

Her mother, Holly, finished clearing the table and said, "Well, have you ever thought about asking THEM to play?"

"It's not that easy, Mom!" Noelle said. "I mean, have you ever been the new kid?"

"Oh, yes, well, about a thousand years ago," her mother said. "But I was lucky. My nana—your great-grandmother—had a wonderful rag doll named Beatrice. She gave her to me so I wouldn't be so lonely. Until I made new friends of my own—and even after that—Beatrice was my best friend. I could tell her anything, even my most embarrassing moments, and I always felt safe."

"Whatever happened to her?" Noelle asked.

"I wish I knew, dear," Holly said. "Over the years she just disappeared. I like to think that maybe she is with another child who needed a best friend. But maybe we could use a new rag doll—a new best friend for our new home. Perhaps you should write a letter to Santa asking for one."

"A doll for both of us?" Noelle asked.

"Well, let's just say it's for you," Holly said. "Santa may think I'm a little old for a doll."

"I'm going to write a letter right now," Noelle said.

"That's an excellent idea, dear," her mother said. "Writing is a much better plan that waiting and wishing."

Noelle got paper and her pencil and began to write:

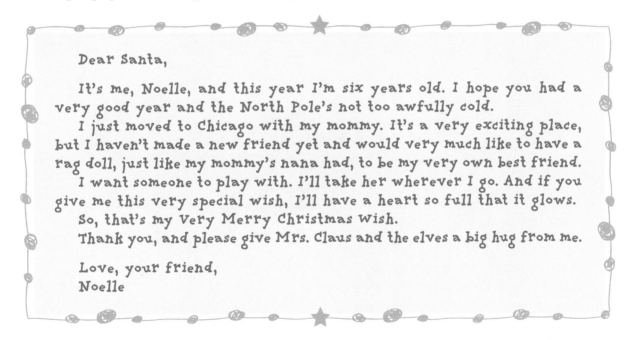

> Dear Santa,
>
> It's me, Noelle, and this year I'm six years old. I hope you had a very good year and the North Pole's not too awfully cold.
>
> I just moved to Chicago with my mommy. It's a very exciting place, but I haven't made a new friend yet and would very much like to have a rag doll, just like my mommy's nana had, to be my very own best friend.
>
> I want someone to play with. I'll take her wherever I go. And if you give me this very special wish, I'll have a heart so full that it glows.
>
> So, that's my Very Merry Christmas wish.
>
> Thank you, and please give Mrs. Claus and the elves a big hug from me.
>
> Love, your friend,
> Noelle

Noelle placed her letter on the front hall table to be mailed the very next day.

CHAPTER SEVEN

WHERE WE BELONG

After Santa and Cookie read Eleanor's letter, Santa said, "I'm troubled by this, my dear. Little girls now want video games and phones and glamorous dolls with cars and houses and clothes and those hair things and glitter for their eyes. I can't remember the last time a little girl asked for a rag doll. This is a most difficult problem. I'm afraid even I don't have a solution for this."

"Nonsense," said Mrs. Claus, shaking her head and giving Santa a kiss on his forehead. "Every problem has a solution. The most important solutions are the ones we have to work harder to find. A letter will come, but until it does, it is our job to make sure that Eleanor knows how very much she is loved. I think I'll start a batch of her favorite cookies."

And, of course, because Cookie was always right, Santa nodded, gave her a kiss on her cheek and said, "Yes, my dear, that's the most important thing."

Just then, Eleanor peeked out from behind the door where she had been standing.

"Oh, but I do know how much you all love me," she said. "What I don't know is why I'm here."

"Eleanor, have you ever thought that maybe you have been a gift to us?" Cookie asked. "You know how sad Santa and the elves and I feel when all the toys leave us on Christmas Eve. Even though we know they are going to wonderful homes, it is so hard to say goodbye. How lucky we are that you have stayed and become part of our North Pole family."

While that did make Eleanor feel special, she couldn't help but blurt out, "But why am I HERE? Shouldn't there have been a letter from a little girl asking for me? I know how careful Clara and Sprinkle and Sparkle are with the list. They would never create a toy without a letter. So why am I here?"

Cookie looked at Santa.

Santa took Eleanor's hands in his.

"Well, Eleanor, I guess it's time for the whole truth," he said. "There was a letter, a lovely letter requesting a special doll. And that's exactly what the elves created when they made you. But just after you came to us, we received another letter from that little girl saying that she had changed her mind and that she was much too old for a doll. She was afraid her friends would make fun of her. You wouldn't have wanted that."

"No, I guess not," Eleanor replied.

"And we couldn't send you to a home where you were no longer wanted," Santa said. "So, we kept you here where you are very much loved."

"So," Eleanor said, fighting back tears, "I wasn't a mistake?"

"A mistake?" Cookie said, giving Eleanor a hug. "Of course not! How could any toy who is loved be a mistake? Let's never hear talk like that again. You are a very special doll and are loved very much by all of us. I like to think that we're all exactly where we're supposed to be when we're supposed to be there. And your place, at least for now, is right here."

"You are loved," Santa said.

"You are family," Cookie added.

"Don't you ever, ever forget that," they told her.

Eleanor didn't know whether to laugh or cry, so she did a bit of both.

"I won't," Eleanor said. "I promise."

The others began to gather for breakfast and the start of another day. And that day was one of Eleanor's happiest days at the North Pole. To know just how much she was loved was a wonderful gift. As they sat by the fire later that night, Eleanor shared the letter and her wish with everyone. She now understood that we should never keep secrets from the people we love the most. As she looked around at her North Pole family, she was sure that it would be a long time before she thought about leaving them again.

And the days passed just as they had for so many years before.

CHAPTER EIGHT

THE LETTER!

One rather quiet day, Eleanor was playing with Twinkle when Sprinkle and Sparkle came running.

"Eleanor! Eleanor!" they yelled. "Come quickly. Santa is looking for you!"

Off they ran to find Santa, who sat with Cookie and Clara by the fire.

"Yes, Santa, what is it?" Eleanor asked when they found him. Santa was flushed with excitement. Cookie and Clara paced about excitedly.

"Good, we're all here," Santa said. "Gather 'round the fire. I have a letter here that I want to read. Clara, thank you for bringing it to me so quickly."

"Of course, Santa!" Clara said. "I had a feeling this was a very special letter."

"A letter?" Eleanor said. "In the middle of the day? It must be very special."

"I think you'll agree that it is," Santa said. "Are we ready?"

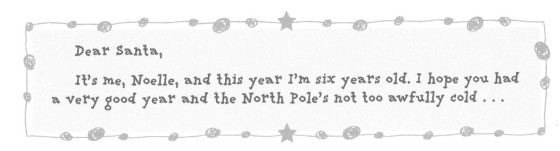

Dear Santa,

It's me, Noelle, and this year I'm six years old. I hope you had a very good year and the North Pole's not too awfully cold . . .

Santa continued, ending with, "So, that's my Very Merry Christmas Wish." He turned and said, "Well, well, well. What do we all think of that?"

Sprinkle could barely contain himself.

"My, my . . . this is exciting news," he said with a gleam in his eye, "but where will we ever find a doll this extra special?"

They all had a very big belly laugh at that.

"Oh, Sprinkle!" Cookie said. "We know EXACTLY where to find that special doll."

Sprinkle and Eleanor laughed hardest of all.

In his most official voice, Santa said, "Clara, what do we know about this Noelle?"

Clara didn't even need her notes.

"Well, we do know that Noelle lives in Chicago with her mommy," she said. "We know that her mommy named her Noelle because it means 'Christmas,' and her mommy just loves Christmas. We also know that she is a very good girl. Oh, and her mother's name is Holly!"

"Holly!" Twinkle shouted with a laugh.

"HOLLY!" everyone shouted in unison.

Santa then looked at Eleanor.

"Well, Eleanor, what do you think?"

Eleanor smiled.

"I think she sounds perfect," she said. "And her name means 'Christmas.' So, just like here, it would feel like Christmas every day."

So, it was settled. Eleanor's very merry Christmas wish had come true at last. Santa gave Eleanor a hug, turned to them all, and said, "This calls for a celebration. Tonight, we'll have a very special dinner and cookies for dessert. Now, everyone, there's lots to do to get ready, so back to work! But first, a toast—to Eleanor and her new best friend and home."

They all raised their cups of hot cocoa in a toast.

"To Eleanor!" they all shouted.

CHAPTER NINE

CHRISTMAS EVE!

ach year, the workshop and kitchen became busier and busier as the holidays approached. And before they knew it, it was Christmas Eve! Just like every Christmas Eve, before and since, there was much excitement and hustle and bustle as Santa prepared for his busy night. But this was the most special Christmas Eve that any of them could remember. Everything was the same, and yet everything was different, for in the midst of it all was happiness for Eleanor but great sadness knowing that she would be leaving them.

There was a final flurry of activity. Eleanor helped Mrs. Claus prepare the sleigh for Santa. They would pack a thermos of hot chocolate, Santa's favorite sandwiches, and some very healthy kale chips. They never packed cookies because Mrs. Claus knows that there will be plenty of cookies left by children—and carrots for the reindeer—all along his magical journey.

Eleanor watched in amazement as the elves packed the sleigh with all of the gifts they had created and wrapped so beautifully. It was quite a sight. The elves formed a line and passed the gifts one by one from the workshop, through the courtyard, and into Santa's sleigh. Eleanor could hardly believe her eyes at how quickly they worked and just how much fun they all had.

Then it was time. All of the gifts had been packed except one very special gift: Eleanor. This Christmas Eve, Eleanor would not wave goodbye to the toys that were leaving. This year, SHE would be waving goodbye and leaving.

"Are you ready, Eleanor?" Sprinkle asked as helped her into the sleigh. "You can have my seat this year, right next to Santa."

Eleanor noticed that Sprinkle seemed to have something in his eye. Funny, now it seemed SHE had something in her eye. She wiped away a tear.

"Sprinkle, is that something in your eye?" Eleanor said. "Are you crying?"

"I'm not crying. You're crying," Sprinkle said.

"Well, I'll admit it," Cookie said. "I am crying!"

"Gosh, everyone, now that my wish has come true, I'm just as happy as I am sad," Eleanor said. "But that doesn't make any sense, does it?"

"Of course it does, my dear," Cookie said. "Sometimes we have to say 'Toodle-loo' to one thing to make way for another. But remember, change is not the end. Now you'll have your new home, your new best friend, AND your North Pole family. Because no matter how long gone or far away, the people you love are always in your heart."

"Gosh, I'll miss you all so much," Eleanor said. "Thank you for EVERYTHING! And especially for teaching me how to wear white boots."

Clara laughed and hugged Eleanor.

"Oh, you did that on your own," she said. "You're stronger than you know. Now, off you go, and I don't want to see YOUR name on the wrong side of the Naughty-or-Nice List."

"Eleanor," Cookie said, wiping a tear from her eye. "My wish, our wish, is that you are always happy."

And then, just like that, it was time to go. Sprinkle and Sparkle climbed aboard, Santa gave a "Ho ho ho," and the reindeer took them up, up and away.

Cookie and Clara waved until the sleigh was up in the air and completely out of sight.

And what a flight it was.

Eleanor couldn't believe how high the sleigh could fly and how fast the reindeer could carry them. Sprinkle and Sparkle knew every chimney, and Santa was so quick about his work.

Finally, there it was—the Chicago skyline. It was very different from the North Pole, with its tall buildings and beautiful lake. She knew she was going to love it here!

They landed with a thud on the rooftop of Noelle's home. Eleanor could barely contain her excitement. As Santa scooped her from the sleigh, she suddenly realized she now had to say goodbye to the reindeer and Sprinkle and Sparkle.

And to Santa himself.

"Let's not dillydally, Eleanor," Santa said kindly. "You have a new home to explore, and Sprinkle, Sparkle, and the reindeer and I have much yet to do."

With a final hug for Sprinkle and for Sparkle, and with a wave to the reindeer, *whoosh!* Down the chimney she went.

"Here you are, Eleanor," Santa said. "Your new home."

"Oh my, it's just beautiful, isn't it?" Eleanor said. "I mean, it's nothing like the North Pole, but it just feels like home."

"Now remember, one peek at Noelle and then into the gift box you go," Santa said. "Those are the rules: no gifts until Christmas morning. Oh, but I will make one little exception. Here you go, my dear."

Santa handed her a present that was oh-so-beautifully wrapped.

"A present?" Eleanor said. "For me? But, Santa, you've already given me my merry Christmas wish."

"Well, one little gift couldn't hurt," Santa said. "Go ahead."

Eleanor opened the gift to find a pair of gleaming white boots.

"Oh, Santa!" Eleanor cried. "White boots! Just like Clara's. How did you know?"

"Well," he said, "I am Santa Claus, you know."

"Thank you, Santa," Eleanor said. "I'll love them always. And I'll love you and Cookie and all of my North Pole family always. I'm the luckiest rag doll in the whole wide world."

"Well, off I go," Santa said, as he turned away. "I have many stops to make. Be very happy, Eleanor, and know that your North Pole family will think of you always. Remember, no matter how far away friends go, they are never far away in our hearts. And, of course, I'll be back to check on you every Christmas Eve."

Eleanor heard the *whoosh!* of the sleigh as it lifted into the air and on its way.

CHAPTER TEN

A NEW HOME!

In the complete silence, Eleanor realized that, for the first time in her life, she was alone. There was no Santa, no Cookie, no Clara, no Sprinkle or Sparkle or Twinkle.

"So," Eleanor thought, trying to feel brave, "here I am. My new home. I guess I'd better take a look around."

She wandered through the living room and into the kitchen, and then, there SHE was, sleeping soundly in her beautiful bed—her new best friend. Noelle! Eleanor could hardly wait to meet her. But . . . *Rules are rules!* Eleanor thought, as she went back to the living room and climbed into the gift box under the tree to wait patiently for Christmas morning.

Finally, Eleanor heard voices and footsteps, and after what seemed like a lifetime, there she was. Noelle lifted Eleanor from the gift box and said, "Mommy, Mommy, look! Santa brought me a rag doll! Isn't she perfect, Mommy? Isn't she perfect?"

Holly looked surprised as she checked the gift box and tag. Noelle opened the envelope and read the letter from Santa.

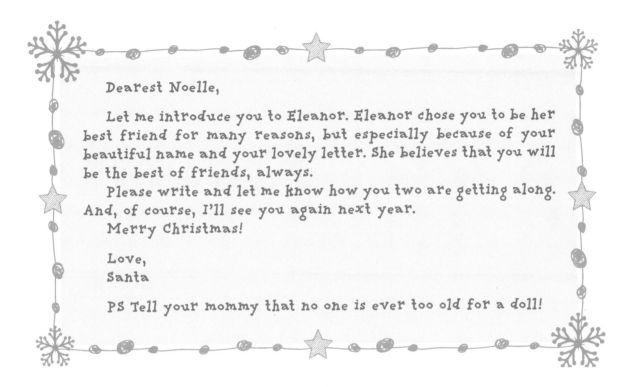

Dearest Noelle,

Let me introduce you to Eleanor. Eleanor chose you to be her best friend for many reasons, but especially because of your beautiful name and your lovely letter. She believes that you will be the best of friends, always.

Please write and let me know how you two are getting along. And, of course, I'll see you again next year.

Merry Christmas!

Love,
Santa

PS Tell your mommy that no one is ever too old for a doll!

"Mommy, Mommy, her name is Eleanor!" Noelle exclaimed. "She's just perfect, isn't she, Mommy?"

Holly took the note from Eleanor and read it, then re-read the surprising "PS" several times.

"Yes, darling, she's perfect," Holly said with a smile. "Welcome home, Eleanor. You are a very merry Christmas wish come true."

Beginning that Christmas morning and every day from then on, Noelle and Eleanor were very best friends. Of course, Eleanor missed her friends at the North Pole and thought about them every single day. But now she had her very own home and her very own best friend. What could be better than that?

CHAPTER ELEVEN

ELEANOR'S NEW ADVENTURES BEGIN

Every year, just as he promised, Santa would come down the chimney. He and Eleanor would visit and have the cookies and milk that Holly had left for him. Santa always had a special gift for Eleanor from the elves, Cookie, and Clara.

And the most special gift of all: Santa gave Eleanor a new recipe from Cookie so that she and Noelle could bake cookies just the way Eleanor had done at the North Pole. Eleanor gave Santa the letters she had carefully written to each of her friends letting them know about her life with Noelle—and how much she missed them.

Much too quickly, Santa would have to hug her goodbye, and up the chimney he went. As she heard the reindeer lift the sleigh up, up and away, she stood at the window, waved, and said, "Thank you, Santa, for making my very merry Christmas wish come true."

And Santa would wink, smile, wave, and, with a "Ho ho ho" and the sound of sleigh bells leading the way, he would head out into the night making Christmas wishes come true for good little girls and good little boys—and good little toys—everywhere.

John Michael Downs
Illustrator

December 17, 1936–October 21, 2019

John Downs created Eleanor with an effortless stroke of his pen,
a splash of color, and a sense of whimsy. His enchanting illustrations brought Eleanor's story to life.
I am sorry that he is not with us in person to see the final result.

Rather than try to find another artist to mimic or complement his creations,
or put his beautiful illustrations in a drawer to gather dust and bring in someone new,
I decided to allow the reader's imagination to fill in the blanks
on those characters not fully realized—the best way to share his vision,
to honor his contribution and celebrate his legacy.

I am sure that John would approve.

Denise McGowan Tracy

Denise McGowan Tracy was born in a magical place called Chicago, in a time before cell phones, when tablets were made of paper. She lives a fairy-tale life that includes spending time with wonderfully talented people who can sing, act, dance and tell stories. And, of course, some villains and plot twists. Many of these talented people are her very good friends, so Denise spends countless hours in theaters watching make-believe come to life. When she is not attending theater or performing on a cabaret stage, she is producing events and entertainment, including the stage adaptation of this book, *Eleanor's Very Merry Christmas Wish: The Musical*. She is currently living happily ever after with her husband, Ed, in their castle along Lake Michigan where they watch the moon and stars and make their wishes every night.

SPECIAL THANKS!

I am grateful to John Koehler/Koehler Books for assistance in publishing this book and to everyone involved with producing its stage adaptation, Eleanor's Very Merry Christmas Wish—The Musical.

www.eleanorswish.com

Make Your Wish!

CPSIA information can be obtained
at www.ICGtesting.com
Printed in the USA
LVHW071445051120
670810LV00009B/421

9 781646 633029